The deer had his nose
in the air.
"A man is near," said
the deer.
"I fear men."

The deer came to a
road.
The deer did not see
the jeep.
The man in the jeep
did not see the deer.

As the deer ran in
the road, the jeep
hit him.
The man in the jeep
did not mean to hit
the deer.

The deer hit a pile of
wire near the side of
the road.
The deer got up and ran.

The deer had a cut on
his ear and a big cut
on his rear leg.

The deer was weak
and sore and in a lot
of pain.

"I hear a man," said
the deer.
"I am not safe here,
but I can not get up."

The man came up to
the deer.
"I need to take care of
you," said the man.
"I will take you home."

The man got the deer
home.
He had the deer lie
on a rug near the fire.

"I can take care of his
leg," said the man.
The man tore up a rag.
"I can use this to tie
up your sore leg,"
said the man.

Late in the week, the
man said, "Your leg
is fine. I can not keep
you here. You need to
go home."

The man did not dare
let the deer get tame.
A deer has to fear
men to be safe.
But the deer liked
the man.

The man and the deer
were on a hike near
the lake.
"I will not take him
home," said the man.

"It is time for you to go
home," said the man.
The deer did not run.
The deer came up to
the man and made a
sad moan.

"Run," said the man.
"See that deer near
the lake?"
His deer ran to the
deer near the lake.

The man had to wipe a
tear as his deer got to
the lake.
"Keep safe, deer,"
said the man.